Copyright@Gloria Oluchi John, 202

All Rights Reserved.

ISBN: 9798837977114

VAMPIRE AUNT

(EPISODE 1)

In the wee hours of the morning when every living busy soul still want to catch some bits and pieces of sleep , a beautiful woman in her middle thirties was lasciviously fondling the private area of a young lad not more than twelve years of age .

Her large bourbon eyes shone with mischief, her lips kept navigating through every lines of her mouth as though it harbours sweetness.

"Michael you belong to me now , if I don't have your father forever , I shall have you forever "   Purred the insane woman .

The young lad obviously seemed sapped and lethargic, his half closed eyes was bereft of life . His mouth seemed as though they were moving and yes sir , they were really moving hence he was mouthing some unintelligible words .

"Aunty please , Aunty please ,Aunty please"

Were the only intelligible words that could be picked from his gibberish .

The young woman continued with the ungodly activity , it was asif her whole life depended on it , She turned deaf ears to his pleas and instead giggled a reply , she let out a conspiratory smile , a wicked glint adorned her beautiful eyes.

The glint of devilment in her eyes lingered, she gave the wet bloody whip that Sat obediently beside her a contented stare asif to say " Hey whip ! you have done well"

She grasped the whip and it suddenly went sprawling on the floor from her hands, she bent her head and began to work her lips on the fountain of blood that angrily trickled about

on the young boy's body,
she licked on ravenously in
abandon,determined to bath
him with her tongue.

The blood indeed seemed like an
ambroisa for she never
wanted to stop working her
lips on the poor lad's body .

Finally the Crazy lady stopped
ravishing his body with her
lips and leveled up to
another uncanny deed, her
eyes suddenly shone with
desire and she rented her
customary black nightie
into unruly pieces which
rendered her provocatively
naked safe for the black
handkerchief which was
tied on her head . She
climbed over the poor boy
and lasciviously enveloped
his lethargic body with hers
, then the rest was history
....

....
:........................
....

Two lovers were seen sleeping
comfortably
in a king sized bed, their legs
entwined into each other's ,
they slept on in oblivion
and silence, silence So
strong that the rasping of

their breaths merged into a sweet rhytym.

Natasha was the first to be stired into reality, she flickered her eye lids open , blinked for the upteempth time. Her eyelids , big and captivating was a plethora of mists. She tilted her head to one side and stared at the handsome face of the Adonis like young fella sleeping next to her , she let out a shy smile and muttered inaudibly.

"Spending the weekend with you is heaven honey "

She placed a light kiss on his right cheek and made to saunter out of the bed when she looked at him again .

"Surely this god sleeping next to me is passionate about me too "   She muttered again in a bid to reassure herself of the virility of their 3 months old relationship Which surprisingly had turn out strong .

She kept on staring at her Adonis like lover , with silent tears coursing down her cheek. She placed her dainty hand on his hair and stroked the trendils effeminatly, those dainty fingers navigated his hair , when they got to his scarred body , they started to twitch .

"My Poor Michael it seems didn't have it all rosy while growing up "   She thought

"And who on earth Will have the heart to administer such scary and uncanny scar on a young man's body ? holy Moses !   Her though lingered with unanswered questions .

" Oh ! he is such an enigma and beautiful, I can stare at him all day "

She muttered ....

Natasha's hands found their ever curious way back to the tendrils of his ruffled hair and phew! asif on cue his eyelids flew open.

This startled the poor lady ,her eyes almost bulged out of their sockets   ,her   almost protruding eyes found his cool gaze but they were as red as stoplight, their eyes locked and for a nano second , the world was really revolving around them .

....

....

....

Natasha felt like she have been caught red handed with her hands in a cookie jar.Her eyes was red with embarrassment, she made to remove her twitching hands from his ruffled hair when he skilfully grasp her hand and encircled it in his big sturdy ones.

suddenly, he climbed over her so Suddenly he climbed over her So that she Will be trapped under him , she gasped and stared on, wide eyed like a New born infant but this time in bewilderment ,

The young man noticed her discomfort and Smiled knowingly , he seemed to be amused at her discomfort ,he gave out a smirk and nodded his head In satisfaction , asif he just finished a herculean task.

" Babe, you look beat "   He said, whilst releasing that

his killer smile which every woman Will kill for .

" Errrrr....mm ......mm"

Natasha stuttered Nervously ,her wit scattered and words waning, still clearly flustered and embarrassed at being caught.

"you twerp ! what were you thinking staring at him like a teenager, gosh! you barely know him that much , get a grip on yourself girlie, he might take you for a push over!

Natasha thought , admonishing herself.

Asif he knew what she was thinking, Michael's smirk deepened, he tilted his head obviously enjoying her discomfiture.

"Errr.... honey I thought you would be very mad at me because you don't like being touched especially on those scars"

she said , with a catch in her voice.

....
....

Michael suddenly stiffened at the mention of the word "Scar" .

Natasha became stiff under him, dreading what would happen next .

He skillfully climbed out of the bed and stared at her with a tinge of sadness in his
eyes, every sinew and lines of his scarred but beautiful body bespoke pain.

Annoyance was etched on his handsome face, he glowered at her . Anger, pain, hatred , revenge and everything bad was glaring on his handsome face .

For a nano second, Natasha saw his muscle tighten and fear gripped her .Her eyes suddenly became a mist of tears, she held her breath in trepidation , bracing her self for the worst.

 " He won't hit me , he won't ever hit me , I know for sure that he loves me "

Thus went her fragile thought Which bolstered her confidence ..

She willed herself to climb out of the bed, her flowing nightie a big contrast to her fair skin colour.

To her surprise , Michael hastily grabbed his shirt and skillfully put it on so that it complements the boxer briefs he wore , he made to say something when the now relieved and undaunted Natasha mouthed in a gutsy tone , just in a bid to fish out the truth ,years of practise as a journalist had thought her to always feed her curiosity at all cost ....

"Why do your countenance change whenever I talk about the scars playing tattoo on your body"

Michael combusted with something Natasha could not really decipher, is it panic,fear or anger , she could not really place her hands on it .

Suddenly,she caught a trace of panic on his sad face , at that moment ,he seemed vulnerable with his whole body convulsed with pain.

"O my! did I just catch a mist of tears in his eyes.

she asked herself, obviously bewildered.

"Natasha why, why did u mention the Scar , who are you , why do you always let me off guard , why are you different from the other bitches ,are you the death of me!!!

He thundered , his voice husky with emotions ....

....
....
"Oh my !
Goodness gracious me !
Do men also cry ?
Did I stir out those tears ?
This is unbelievable, am I hallucinating , wow , and what was he saying about bitches ?

Natasha wondered in bewilderment, obviously puzzled . Emboldened by his current disposition, her gutsy self surfaced again .

"And why do you get nervous whenever i made mention your aunty's name ?

Michael's body stiffened, his eyesballs went red like embers , his face became etched with sorrow and a tinge of panic at the mention of his aunt and for the fleestest moment, , he looked like a crestfallen little boy, hot tears uncontrollably streamed out of his eyes.

"why is this particular woman doing this to me , no woman has ever made me this vulnerable except for that old bitch "   He thought frantically

" O boy ! men really do cry ....

Natasha whistled her thought , She hardened her resolve and decided to keep probing him at his weakest moment though scared ....

"Micheal you know you can keep talking to me "   she said in stifled fear .

His unabated silence startled her, she made to run out of the room but thought better of it .....

"My love , I am the only woman you can derive solace from in the world ,talk to me"

She said in a bid to sooth him.

Asif possesed by some unseen forces, Michael took a menacing step forward and regarded her steadily, this made Natasha to retreat in fear. He stopped on his track and scowlded at her, saying nothing .

For an awful moment , Natasha thought he has gone deaf . Prickled with desperation , she ran to him, held his face effeminatly , made sure their eyes locked and thundered bravery with an unladylike scowl .

"Talk to me you jerk ! you are driving me nut , gosh !

"why would i ?

The stoic man replied with a scowl ...

"Because I love you sincerely not your money you idiot!

She thundered back with a faltering voice and this time around navigated into an outburst of tears ....

And it was asif Michael's demons has finally been stired, his eyes, a semblance to midnight searched hers , truly Natasha have never seen someone glower this hard in her entire life and coming from him , she was baffled for the alien look in his eyes bespoke panic and murder, truly she have never seem him this mad .

She started to move forward in a bid to touch his arm in order to affirm his sanity when he retreated and frantically stretched his hand in a bid to stop her .

"Now get out ! Away with you ! you nosy woman ! before I do something drastic to you!
what makes you think you can pass your boundary , because I allow you to see those scars ? your lot reek of evil! you are evil and nosy!

"What !

Natasha tensed .

" Did you just call me evil "

She said , shaking vigorously with hurt ....

Ignoring her , Michael continued with his tirades ..

"Just get out, your lot are nothing but bags of evil "

The puzzled Natasha just stood rooted on a spot, scarcely able to believe what She is hearing ....She decided to control her anger and said with an icy calm ...

" Michael I am not evil, I can help yo......

"No ! bitch I don't need help , especially not from a wanton woman .....gosh! wantons all over me !

"Goodness me! he is crazy, he surely needs help"

She muttered inaudible ,lost in her erratic thought .Then to her surprise, he jolted her awake, away from her sad reverie..

" She ripped me off a conventional life, She is a husk of a woman, a mistake to womanhood ,She is a wanton, she.......

" Who is she !!

Natasha thundered in exasperation, thrusting her face into his ,desperate for an amiable answer ....

" My aunt !

He thundered back in indignation
........:

EPISODE 2

What!

Natasha couldn't register What she
just heard , for all she know
, Mrs Priscilla Drake
Ejiofor , a beautiful
wealthy and famous
senator in the house of
assembly is the Nicest
woman in the whole
universe..

with an icy calmness and a face
wreathed in smile , she
thrusted her face into his
,held his face effeminatly
and remarked with a voice
that's as smooth as milk.

"But mich, your aunt should love
you so dearly ,i mean you
are family "

" O just shut it , you wench !
What the fuck do you know
!

He retorted , not after removing
her hands from his face ,

making it seem like her hands has scalded his face .

"Buh mich that's too hars......

"She made me a psychopath , can't you see Tasha , am a big mess "

Michael interrupted and kept up with his tirade , not bothered if he has her audience or not .

"I am a lovelorn man, I don't deserve to love or to be loved , I have done terrible stuffs in my life , all thanks to that bitch, my life is ruined , in fact all women are Scum !!

His last words inflamed Natasha, anger welled up in every sinew of her being, she glowered at him and shouted back .

" How dare you insult my specie Micheal !

" Hahaha... your specie indeed !

He growled back with a tinge of sarcasm in his voice and a smirk .Unnerved by his retort, she continued , this time with an icy calm .

"Your Aunt Mrs Priscilla   Drake
           Ejiofor is a philanthropist,
           she has changed the lives
           of   many   with   her
           benevolence . Mind you
           she is a public personality ,
           gosh ! Do you want to ruin
           her Political career !

   " Political Career indeed "

Michael Snorted ...

Natasha ignored him and continued .

"Just in case you don't know that
           Your wonderful aunt gave i
           and other indigent youths
           scholarships   right   from
           secondary   school   to
           university   level.Gosh!
           Michael even after the
           death of your parent , She
           took you in as a Son and
           made   you   the   richest
           bachelor in portharcourt, a
           mogul and C.E.O of Mich
           enterprises,the   media
           doesn't lie, now tell me
           what you want from the
           poor woma......."

   " Hahahaha ",,

Michael went into another outburst
           of hysteric laughter ..

"Tasha O Tasha , you are Just a naive little princess"

He said with a trace of sarcasm in his voice .

"She made you all believe these craps,goodness gracious me! all females are snakes, she In particular is a crazy witc..........

This inflamed Natasha ,she went berserk and impulsively mouthed ..

"Just shut it , you ungrateful brat, you have always had everything at your becks and calls ...You are just a mistake of a man ,a shame to manhood, an ungrateful bra.....

Before she could complete her sentence , a hot slap perilously landed on her face, Natasha went pepper red with shock , the slaps were like a bucket of snowy cold water poured on her pride.

" yo..u sla..pp...ed me "

She stuttered in shock whilst clasping her arms to her bosom and retreating slightly in a bid to wade

off another slap just incase
it's coming her way again.

Michael glowered at her and said
with ire which was evident
in his voice .

"you flew too close to my Sun, I
warned you but your
stubbornness is indomitable
i guess "

An awkward silence loomed over
the big master bedroom
.Suddenly Natasha's eyes
became glacial and icy cold
with rage and like a knife
she cut through the silence.

" I am leaving you "

she spewed .....

" What !

It was asif the world had come
crashing on Michael's head,
the words " I am leaving
you" was a wake up call for
him, his heart began to beat
in a frantic pounding tattoo.

" Na...ta..sha, yo..u can't do th..is
to me"

He stuttered.....

For a second his beautiful face
became a resemblance to

that of a guilty child .He suddenly seemed creastfallen and contrite , unbelievable tears blurred his vision ...

"O I thought this particular woman is here to stay , O GOD but I love this woman, she is different from the others. Her shy smiles during love making , her feisty but effeminate nature, her intelligence , her wits, her culinary skills, her understanding is all I want in a woman ....O am a mess ,why did I hit her ? O aunty why !

Indeed these were the thoughts that were rummaging his erratic mind .

"Michael I need to pack my stuffs!

Natasha practically shouted , her eyes also was decorated with mists of tears..

This shook Michael out of his sad riverie, he suddenly knelt down before her in
Sobriety , something he seemed to have never done to anyone except his crazy aunt.

"Angel please don't leave me , your departure will convey darkness to my already meaningless life, it's been three months but it feels like three years , it's a sign that you are a special made , wonderfully made for this messed man   , I really didn't know what came over me "

He said whilst crying profusely at her feet like a penitent lover...

"See micheal, I am not going to succumb , not for all the tea in china. You are obviously not ok, you need psychological help, am tired of trying to be a saviour , you don't need me"

She replied , her resolve hardened .

Palpable silence radiated in the room, Michael looked up in supplication , asif searching for divine intervention .

"Tasha, you are the only woman that makes me lose my guard, can't you See?am all over you like bee to honey . you are the only woman who cares about me, your words of endearment to me are like mannas from heaven , believe me Tasha, I have never been in love until I met you , your name is like a benediction on my lips, please Tasha, I know am a messed man , pls help me, I love you .

Micheal remarked softly with a voice that's laced with fear.

He looked at her expectantly , his face white with anxiety,he dreaded her response and for an awful moment , he thought she was gonna walk out on him.

Tasha retreated , this made perspiration to form on Michael's face like beads, he held his breath in oblivion and kept gawking at her .....

"Gosh ! this feeling felt new, why can't i just dismiss her like I do to the other women, why can't i do away with this particular woman , what is wrong with me ?

Came the tumult of question playing tricks with his mind.

" I won't go on one condition "

Michael was brought back from his sad reverie, he felt relief wash over him like a tidal wave , his blood began to sing in his veins, thruming loudly through his ears.

" O , ok ok ma'am"

He said whilst grinning from ear to ear , his face almost splitting into two , it was wreathed in an innocent smile ...

Natasha regarded him steadily , she tilted her head and smiled,all grudges forgotten. The mists of tears in his eyes brought a melting glow spreading like warm honey through her veins....

"Micheal Eric Okafor, the haughty C.E.O of Mich Entreprises isn't a complete jerk after all, Who would believe he would plead like a baby for a woman's love"

Natasha thought within herself , almost letting out a giggle in the process.

" Err..mm I love you too"

She said almost shyly .....

This made Michael to beam not with surprise this time but with joy, his eyes suddenly lit up like christmass , he skillfully stood up and submerged her in his sturdy embrace ...He heard her sigh deeply in his arms and frowned slightly ...

" What baby ?

He asked with his eyes searching hers .

She looked at him boldly and mouthed ... "If you don't want me to go Michael ,you need to regale me with your story .....

....
          ....

Michael stiffened and blanched , and once again tension radiated in the room ...

"Michael am dead serious this time around"

She said firmly , her resolve hardened ....

" Ermm baby are you trying to blackmail me?

He quizzed softly , careful not to annoy her ...

" No Michael, I just want to get to know my man "   She said whilst pouting her lips petulantly , mimicking a spoilt teenage girl ..

"gosh tasha, you are one stubborn and Loquacious woman" He said , obviously helpless ....

"And that's why I swept you off your feet honey , now if you would start talking sir !

She said whilst winking and mimicking a salute ..With a voice that rose to a crescendo.

Michael stared helplessly at her, obviously in a dilema.

"How can I start to uncover those horrible childhood memories"

He thought frantically ... voices were speaking to him like that of those invisible witches that spoke to Macbeth ...

Natasha stood ever gallantly, Obviously waiting for him to start to uncover the mysteries of his life ...

" Michael am listening "   She said for the umpteenth time , watching his face for every fleeting expression with an awkward calm , biting back the tumult of questions that's threatening to burst out from her mouth. Instead She said softly and hissed ...

"Stubborn Man "

....
....

Those Invisible voices kept playing chess with Michael's mind, and for the fleetest moment , he had a resemblance to Macbeth the legendary king ...

"Hey Micheal, you should tell her , rid your self off this burden , you are no more the little crying teeny weeny helpless boy from yesterday, you are now a full fledged man, Michael talk to her , do tell her "

Said a still small voice , gentle and soothing , not coaxing but leaving him to make a decision ...

"Ha! Michael my guy , do you want to expose the woman who took good care of you

like her own , remember you would have been homeless if it wasn't for her ,and how are you so sure this busy body of a girl won't use it against you remember she is a fucking reporter, a nosy one at that"
A loud voice coaxed him .

"Stop talking to me "

Mummured the confused Michael to Natasha's shock surprise .

She made to say something but shut her mouth like a clam and watched in shocked horror.

The voice continued with it's charades obviously bent on playing tricks with the young man's minds like the witches did to Macbeth the legendary king.

"Besides what does the bible says about forgiving ,dude just forgive your aunt and tell no one what she did to you , after all she is a lone woman and you were there looking so handsome even as a boy , keep those terrible memories locked in your heart , forgive and forget , such is life Michael , be a man !

"No ! I said shut up ! I can't stand the nightmares anymore, i need to talk to someone who understands me better than anyone , I will tell her my story , she understands me , I don't want her to leave me , she is my woman , mine !mine! mine!!

Micheal thundered .

With his whole body twitching , he suddenly hugged the bewildered Natasha, he wrapped protective arms around her like he would do to his mother ...

" Please Tasha don't leave me, I will talk ,I will talk !!

He said softly amidst tears

Natasha's love for him increased , it brought her closer to him like a moth to a flame, his contagious tears puzzled her, she hugged him back tightly , her vision blurred with tears .

"Now ho.ney you will sta...rt talk...ing okkk, am he..re for you "

She stuttered ,obviously perplexed by the monologue he just played out . She freed herself from his sturdy embrace, stood on tiptoe and managed to plant a light kiss on his forehead for he was provocatively tall. He reciprocated her endearing gesture , sniffed like a child, and sat on the edge of the king sized bed , Tasha followed suit , looking at him in anticipation ...

"Ok Tasha , it all happened after my parent died in a ghastly accident"

"O boy !

Tasha muttered under her breath, her eyes bespoke something that's akin to curiousity and horror ....

Michael met her gaze steadfastly and his expression slightly softened ,he let out a pathetic smile and mouthed.

"It all started a month after I moved in with aunty Priscilla.......

EPISODE 3

A young woman in her middle thirties was seen admiring herself vaingloriously before her strange looking gargantuan mirror in the confines of her room ,indeed she was truly beautiful. she let out a smirk which immediately vanished from her beautiful face, she swirled around and accompanied every move with strange chuckles.

Her eyes brown like bourbon was etched with sorrow and bereft of life, her black dress was a sharp contrast to her skin colour but a semblance to her heart . Again she gawked at her reflection in the mirror and smiled with malicious relish, she lumbered forward and caressed the mirror effeminatly as though it's her lover .

Amidst the rosy mood she had the grace to look crestfallen and suddenly began to speak to the mirror but in hush tones......

"Eric ! you broke my heart and cheated on me with my kid

sis, you chosed Nanita over me after using me and since you died I have never really had much luck with the gents safe for my white husband whom I killed in the state and came back home , hahaha ! but it wasn't my fault though, even the court saw it as self defense. Drake tried to kill me first with that damn gun , everyone just keeps hurting me, hahahaha and I hurt them too , hahahaha "

The young lady suddenly halted her monologue and looked around as though she sensed a presence, she nodded her head in the affirmative and continued with her speech .

"Eric all i ever wanted was you , but unfortunately i killed you because I couldn't have you and whatever i can't have, i destroy" Said the cryptic young lady, her eyes glittering with hate ....

" hahahaha how dare you !! She suddenly bellowed

" you shattered me you bastard ! but now you are dead, I

made sure I finished you and
that little bitch , that usurper who took my man , that betrayer !

She bellowed again but this time around accompanied it with malicious relish ...

"You both have met your Waterloo , rest in tormenting peace Eric, rest too in tormenting peace Nanita , my cute little kid Sis ,I pray ghouls feast ravenously on your decaying bodies"   She remarked with a devilish tone.

"Eric honey , Nanita baby , Michael your son is stuck with me , gosh he looks so much like you Eric , now he is gonna live the rest of his miserable life at my mercy for I am the only family he's got, mehhhnnn i will make sure I destroy him, I Will ruin him, I Will ravish him , i Will suck his blood! hahahahaha"

She remarked again with a wicked glint and a tongue that navigated her lips now and then like an hungry reptile ...

She walked seductively to the bed
and grabbed a teddy bear ...

"Micheal baby, your aunty Priscilla
is coming for you , we are
gonna be playing myriad of
games all through your stay
with me, let's see who wins
sweetie..."

She said to the bear and blew a kiss
at the stuffed inanimate
thing, She smirked and
gave it a loud peck on the
cheek, her eyes dancing
with scornful humour...

" Let's see who wins"

She repeated and for the umpteenth
time let out a wicked
laughter, but this time
around it rose to a
crescendo ....

....
              ....
              ....
              ....
              ....

At the darkest hour of the night
when every sane living soul
is oblivious to the world
around them , Priscilla
Jolted awake as though she
was being stired by some
strong forces, her eyes
twinkled with mischief ,

she let out a wicked smile and gave the door an impassive look.

Unsavory thoughts were running through her erratic head , she gingered out of the rather humongous bed and walked regally out of the room like she is about to carry out an honourable deed. She barged into the room opposite her's and gawked at the twelve _year old innocent sleeping boy, she sashayed to his bed and regarded his body with her eyes amorously.

"O! what a handsome boy, he looks so much like his father O Eric, O Eric ...you came back to me "

She whispered salaciously ,obviously jinxed asif on the influence of something.

She suddenly clasped his latent hand and held it firmly and possesively on the soft contours of her bosom so that it squeezes her small sized breast, she began to moan softly whilst mouthing words of endearment.

"Eric please don't let go again, am sorry I was the death of you but i went angry with jealousy , you do magic to me like a sorcerer's wand, your touches are soft like midnight breeeze, Eric why did you chose that little bitch over me, why Eric , why?

The poor lad who had been oblivious of the uncanny activities that had lingered for minutes quickly jolted awake and went into a frenzy when he saw his aunt displaying accross him, he skillfully climbed out of the bed with youthful disposition and stared wide eyed in shock at the crazy woman , his eyes almost protruding out of their sockets.

....
....

The little boy's confused stare roamed her fully clothed body , and with a catch in his voice and a stutter he mouthed....

" A...un..ty, wh..at is all this abo..ut"

Her response was an unintelligent answer which the bewildered boy couldn't decipher.

" Eric I love you "

" Errrmm Aunty that's my daddy's name"

He said and kept staring at her , indecisive of what to do next , he knew there was something strange about this woman , her unusual giggles, her customary black nighties, the strange way in which she looks at him whilst licking her lips asif getting ready to devour a prey, her crazy smirks.

The precocious boy finally decided that she must be really crazy .....

"Mummy , daddy where are you both , I need you both now "

The young boy thought desperately to himself ...

He looked at the door and the crazy lady's gaze followed his, she smiled knowingly and climbed out of the bed , she walked graciously to the door and bolted it, then she held the bunch of keys temptingly in the the air so that it dangles ...

" Come darling , Come take the key"

She said with pretend primness and sincerity...

When he didn't make a move to Come for the key, she walked slowly towards him , bent slightly and thrusted her face into his , she made to plaster a kiss on his mouth   When   he impulsively   maneovered her and ran to the other side of the room , her eyes suddenly went icy with manevolence..

The little boy felt her glare in every sinew of his being and immediately   pleaded, uncertain of what he had done wrong and obviously in a dilemma ..

" Aunty please am sorry "

"Hahahahahahaha ....

Came Priscilla's response ....

Still baffled , he decided to try again ...

" Aunty am............

"Just shut it, you little brat!

She rudely interrupted him, her body seething with anger .....

"Since your father left me for my baby sister , your mother , that bitch , no man has ever made my butterflies to flutter . I want no one but him , he was my first love "

She suddenly stopped talking and bellowed with laughter, startling the little boy so that he jumped and panted mindlessly about in fright .

She Smoothed unruly tendrils of her rich black long hair back into place , tilted her head side ways and gave him her most engaging smile and mouthed with mock politeness .

"Michael boy, shall I have the grace to continue to regale you with our love triangle story ?

The little boy went frantic with worry for his dear life, he looked askance at her with those large eyes laced with fear and uncertainty...

" She must be really crazy " He thought....

" Yea he was meant to be my husband because I met him first but am so glad he came back to me through you , all those years of my AWOL in the United State , Eric and that little bitch were busy making another Eric....That's so sweet"

She Squeaked and jumped like a teenage girl , Michael leapt and stared on in unalloyed shock ..

"Now Michael , you will from now henceforth perform the duties of a lover, just like your father did , O! how i loved that man"

She said her last words rather dreamily and suddenly let out   a   loud   sob. Emboldened by her weak disposition, the little boy chirped in .

"But aunty am not my father Eric am Micheal "

Priscilla ignored him , her sobs lingered.

"Aunty, there are many men out there who would kill to be your man "   He continued

" How dare you , you brat !

She thundered and glowered at him, tendrils of her hair rested almost provocatively on her forehead, malevolence sparkled in her bourbon eyes...

"Can't you see , you are just a spitting image of My First love , Eric reincarnated and came back to me , O My little Eric ...come to me"

She walked towards him which automatically made Michael to retreat....

"Now come over to your aunty, Come and touch me , make me feel like a woman again just like Eric did....

" No ! Aunty No! leave me alone !

The little boy shouted in Exasperation...

Priscilla Stopped on her track , seething with palpable anger and for a Nano second,the atmosphere plunged from hot to rigid.

Then She spoke , breaking through the silence ...

"Ok baby boy , I see you are stubborn, let's do it this way "

She smirked , bent down and fished out a whip (Popular Known as "Koboko") under the bed . On sighting the dreadful object , Michael spontaneously made his way to the previously bolted door , Priscilla swiftly followed him and caught up with him , She dragged him violently to the bed .

At that moment Michael surprisingly became fiesty and pushed her with every ounce of strength that he possess , She staggered and fell on the floor with a thud, screaming at the Zenith of her voice like a wounded polecat ...

" You brat ! how dare you push me !

Michael was caught up in a frenzy at his confused state , he knew he was as dead as a roasted chicken and suddenly felt something hot cascading down his legs, he started to sob.

Priscilla managed to find her feet, She charged towards him and slapped him hard across the face , he fell with a thud and screamed . Still blinded by rage, Priscilla grabbed the wipe ("Koboko") and like a dark threatening entity , She violently tore his shirt (like a demon possessed woman)so that he becomes bare cheated and extremely susceptible to the pains She is about to inflict on him with the wipe.

In a fever of strange excitement she giggled and began to register the devil himself on the boy's body with a strenght she didn't knew she possess , it was asif some stronger forces were abetting her wicked activity on the boy's body .

she saw him jump in shock and immediately her face concorted into a network of evil, it shone brightly with contentment and bits and bits of devilment.

Michael's twelve year old body couldn't quite accustom the pains, the first report of the wipe made him stiffen with shock , at once he knew what pain felt for the first time in his life , he grimaced and accompanied it with screams and shouts for help at the other reports of the wipes .

His angry red blood splattered at every corner of the room , he was practically bathed in his own blood . At the 30th stroke, the contented Priscilla halted the uncanny activity, she heaved a big sigh, carried the now lethargic boy like a bundle and threw him on the bed hence staining the duvet with blood .

She bent beside him and licked her lips as though she is getting ready to eat a sumptuous meal , she bent her head and her lips disgustingly ravished the trickle of blood that cascaded his body like it was a sumptuous meal .She suddenly stopped licking his blood and let out a contented smile , his blood formed a weird moustache under her nose.

She climbed over him , already fantasizing how she would

ravish her supposed lover "
(Eric) sexually in her
mind's eye and for the
umpteenth time she
smirked and reached For
his pyjamas (trouser) .

"Eric honey , finally I gat you ,
you are mine ,forever mine
, always mine "

She mouthed Salaciouly , her eyes
dark with desire....

" Always mine "

She repeated and chuckled
loudly........

EPISODE 4

Miss Kanu Sashayed into the
exquisite looking lecture
hall, looking all ravishing
and dashing as ever.
Catwalking into the lecture
hall every day is one
amongst her ridiculous
idiosyncrasies which
clearly irks the student but
they kept their opinions to
themselves.

No one want to be found in the
black book of the haughty
young lecturer and after all,
their apathy towards her

will do them no good because as freshers they need every Mark they can get to build up solid grade points (GP)

Miss kanu glory in their stare each time she catwalks into the lecture hall,She knew some of the ladies admires her but wouldn't dare to approach her out of fear , she loves that fact that the students fears her .

She haughtily wiped out an invisible dirt from her rather expensive tailored suit with an arrogant swift of the hand.

Being a great Observer, she rather hurriedly studied the countenance of the one hundred and twenty students each and a trace of a wicked smirk kissed her lovely sculptured face .

Palpable Silence welled up in the lecture hall so that the breathing of each student could be heard ,at that moment, miss kanu felt so powerful , she made to take an over confident and imperious gait to the white marker board when the wicked smile plastered on her face suddenly vanished and was replaced with a deep frown , for an awful moment , everyone held their breath ....

"O boy , who will get into her black book today " Thought the class course representative.

" Hey ! you stand up !

She bellowed in command and pointed towards a very handsome young teenage boy who shouldn't be more than sixteen years of age but looked muscular and older .To her chagrin the boy hesitated and remained glued to his seat , he too was boiling in silent wrath ...

"Bitch , why point at me of all the one hundred and twenty student in this lecture hall "

He thought angrily..

Miss Kanu felt her pride being prickled ,she went berserk and bellowed again.

"You bastard! are you deaf or something,I said stand up !

Again the young man hesitated for a moment and reluctantly

stood up , fury was emanating from every pore of his being , he stifled the urge to retort back and was forced to bit back sharp retorts in answer to her scathing remarks.

"The nerve of you , you were chewing a gum in my class and still ignored me , I don't know why they still give bastards like you admission into this prestigious and expensive school "

" Eweeeeeehh!!!

Came the raucous shouts of the students.

The raucous of shouts and exclamations lingered , some student gasped in disbelief, others laughed, which indicated that they aren't surprised by her harsh tirades.

"Shut your traps you devilike Charlattans, you incorrigible brats, you uncouth dumb heads, you lethargic and quaint naysayers, you stupefied phenomenas, you twerps, you dimwits "

The raucous sounds of "Haaaa !
Ewoooooooo ! yeeeee !
Mad   oooooooo   !
Eweeeeehhhhhh." Rented
the air.

Those were the sounds some brave
ones amongst the student
made , the mischievous
ones resort to roars of
laughter while the " I too
knows" amongst them only
smiled knowingly asif the
bombs Miss Kanu just
threw was just a pieces of
cake for them .

The teenage boy in question
tightened his fist in
indignation , every lines
and sinews of his body
stifled the urge to lurch
forward and punch her
cheeky face but suddenly a
wicked thought ran into his
head . A smile lit up his
face like Christmas and like
a miracle, the scowl in his
face vanished as though it
was never there .

" I sure do know how to handle
brazen bitches like you"
He muttered under his
breath and smirked.

"I sure will give you the taste of
your own pain, the way I
do to cheeky beautiful

women like you" His cryptic thought lingered and a lascivious smile travelled accross his face, he suddenly realized that myriad of curious eyes were gawking expectantly at him.

He decided to fake nonchallance towards the lecturer's unethical tirades in order to mirror the tension that was boiling in the lecture hall.He glanced towards the lecturer's direction and mouthed in an unnoticeable mock apology .

" O yes ma'am, i am sorry I didn't hear you ma'am"

"Yes of course you are obviously daft and deaf"

Came the rude response of Miss Kanu who obviously was glorying in the fact that she controls one hundred and twenty teenage students.

" What is your name ? She quizzed...

" I am Michael Eric Okafor ma'am" Replied Michael , the facade of a smile still plastered on his face .

" Michael"

She purred his name softly like a cat whilst giving him a flirtatious look ,those who noticed pretended not to and smiled knowingly, others looked on in oblivion .

"Ok Mr deaf ears, you may have your seat that you so much desire"

She said with a tinge of sarcasm in her voice ..

Roars of laughter exploded in the lecture hall , Michael remained unnerved and just kept up with the pseudo smile that remained plastered on his face , he gave a slight mock bow which everyone mistook to be respect and obediently Sat down , his gesture was accompanied with an elongated

"aaawwwwwwwwwwwww wwwwwwwwnnnnnnnnnnn"

which emanated mostly from the girls and some silly boys. . Miss kanu felt flustered and blushed slightly .

"Ok ok, now everyone decorum please!! 'She shouted.

"Today am going to be taking you on a new course which is Eng 101, I am going to be giving you all the course outline "

"Ok Ma" Came the hearty chorus of the student .

"And you Mr deaf ears , the next time you play the notorious deaf ear syndrome on me again, I will send you out of my class , understood !

" Yes ma'am" He replied sharply ....

The class again went into a row of uncontrollable laughter whilst the chicky lecturer sashayed out of the lecture hall like she always do.

"Woman ! you are dead meat ?

The inflamed Michael muttered under his breath whilst glaring at her retreating figure.........

EPISODE 5

Weeks passed by in a flourish and rush of activities, everyone went about their normal duty of going for classes during the day and sleeping peacefully at night. But one faithful night stood out for the haughty female young lecturer , it was a night she was ever going to remember even in death.

....
                                '
....'................
....

A very male looking shadow walked quietly in tiptoes into the exquisite large living room which screams wealth and affluence, he quietly climbed the long unending stairs but swiftly like the legendary spider man and skilfully opened the door to the room which he suspected must belong to the "bitch" which he self righteously calls her and behold he sighted her lithe body lying peacefully on the rather expensive looking mahogany bed.

Michael Smiled , licked his lips and lumbered forward with soft easy steps . Finding her wasn't difficult, sneaking into the back of her car and waiting patiently wasn't difficult either ..

"Careless woman " He snorted under his breath ...

He gave her a dark long look and clenched his fist until his knuckles showed white, the sight of her made his blood to run in swirling rivulets of liquid fire.

He fished out a small knife from his back pocket , gave it an impassive stare and suddenly burst into a row of hysteric laughter .

This gesture jolted Miss Kanu awake, obviously she was stired by his laughter, she stared wide eye in shock at the threatening entity that stood over her, obviously stupefied.

On sighting the perilious little knife that stayed plastered in his twitching hands , she let out deafening scream .

"Common shut it , you bitch !

The outraged Micheal bellowed......

"You bitch ! He repeated ..

"The nerve of you to openly embarrass and flirt with me, you really had your field day last week at the lecture hall , running your smelly mouth like an untrained parrot !   He snarled ...

"O please , don't kill me , am still a young lady , I have learnt my lessons , as you can see I am very rich , please take whatever you want , my family is wealthy, my father own the bigge......."

"Just shut it ! you proud lady , do i look hungry to you ? I don't want your damn money , I just want to ravish you baby , just as your eyes ravished me the other day, mehn ! I saw that flirtatious look in your eyes , I know you want me too bitch, just admit it now and we would be in cloud nine baby "

He said and blew a fake kiss at her , his eyes dark with lustful desires.

"O please , that was a mistake , I am engaged to be married next month to the son of the minister of infor......."

" Will you keep quiet , you slut!!
He thundered

"O I hate this particular bitch" He
muttermed under his breath
..

Miss kanu shifted uncomfortably in
her bed , beads of sweat
cascaded every contours of
her body , she was
obviously in a frenzy and
sobbed frantically .

"How dare you humiliate me in
front of the entire clas , I
saw you glory in it you
cheap slut! you dare prickle
my ego" He snarled

"O ! I never meant to hurt you , am
so so sorry , i was ju....."

" Shhhhhhhhh "   He
interrupted again for the
umpteenth time ..

A sudden wicked glint sparkled in
his eyes and his eyes
roamed her body from the
tendrils of her hair to the
beautiful sight of her
chocolate coloured thighs
,he was obliged to content
himself with yanking off
her skimpy nighties from
her body.

"Now whore , be a good girl and
spread your two bitchy legs
"

"Ha ! please don't do this to me "

Pleaded the panic stricken lady

" I say spread your legs !

She jumped with a start in
trepidation and made to
scurry out of the room
when the outraged Michael
dragged her by the hair
threw her on the bed like a
bundle .

"'You whore ! I am trying hard to
be nice and easy on you but
goodness gracious ! you are
pushing me !

He snarled

Miss kanu ignored him and stood
up, her resolve now
hardened . She suddenly
became feisty and kicked
him on the groin, he went
sprawling on the floor ,
writhing in pain and
cursing hard . Miss kanu
made a mistake of
frantically rummaging her
suitcase for her car key
while Michael's Snarl still
rented the air .

He finally got his bearing and dragged her hair again ,this time around , it was accompanied with a piping hot slap , her vision suddenly became blurry with tears ,she screamed and fell into the bed once again obviously weak from the unabated struggle .

Michael smiles wickedly , climbed over her and enslaved her in his tight hold , her kicks , scratches and bites were a piece of cake to him , he had received more than that in recent years. He finally had his way with her and felt powerful. Every hard thrust Into her ignited her screams, screams so deafening it made Michael much more powerful ,he rode on like a king , a wicked amorous king I would say ....

....
        ....

" You jerk ! you will never get away with this !

came the sharp retort of a ruffled looking woman to the retreating back of the teenage boy who was on the verge of departing the room .

If only she had known that those angry retorts will be the death of her she would have kept mute and just let the crazy psychopath leave in peace .

His precocious body stiffened and became etched with anger , it took him every ounce of civility not to rush towards her and ghoulishly Stab her with the glittering little knife clasped protectively in his right hand .He swirled around so that he is facing her and slowly walked towards the bed, his body emanated contempt , his dark eyes burned precariously with ire, he glared at her and finally mouthed ..

"You contemptible woman ! you could have shut your mouth but you didn't , I sure will get away with whatever shit I did to you and will soon do to you "

This made trepidation to rush through Miss kanu's bones, she shivered in fright .Michael let out a smirk obviously enjoying her discomforture. With an easy swift of the hand , he grabbed her by the hair and violently dragged her out of the bed ,her cry of agony ripped him to the bones and fueled his anger.

Emboldened by her perpetual plea ,he became charged . With easy moves of his right hand , he slit her wrist with the dreadful object in his sturdy hands and smiled knowingly because he had carried out such uncanny deed a million times .

Angry red blood like wine gushed out of her wrist, her deafening screams infuriated him the more , he slapped her hard across the face and for the umpteenth time violently grabbed her hair . A wicked scowl obdurately plastered his handsome face , he thrusted his face into hers and spewed with all seriousness.

"If you as well again permit your smelly mouth to run riot like that of a hungry mosquitoe, I Will find you again and kill you at a go"

He slowly gave her a light mock kiss on the forehead with pretense   gentlemanliness and said again with a tinge of sarcasm in his voice .

"Thank your stars bitch , bloody murder isn't in my agenda tonight, otherwise I would have stabbed you to death , but am a changed person now "

"You bastard !   The almost unconscious lady shouted but with a weak voice .

"You Will pay for this , you Will pay for this , I Will make you pa......

She stopped midway and fainted .

"haaaaaa haaaaaaaaa, yea bitch, in your grave, make it through the morning or die trying "

The young man said sardonically.

He carefully and meticulously placed the knife in her injured hand and hurriedly wrote a short suicide note , he tucked the note in a big textbook but in a way that it Will be visible and noticeable by the authority .

He looked at the gloves he wore and muttered to himself with a big smile hugging his face .

"Mich boy ! You nah sharp
guy"

He remarked in victory with a
wicked beam .

He walked towards the door and
was about leaving the room
when he gave the almost
lifeless body behind him a
last glare.

"You flew too close to my sun and
you got what you ordered
for bitch" He spat

He wore his hoodie and quietly left
the room and the house as
though he was never there
....

EPISODE 6

At Nineteen , Michael had already
blossomed into a man , he
beats the older guys to it
with his biceps, triceps ,
height , full beards and
wisdom , and with the
ladies he had the midas
touch .

A mere wink get the ladies
scurrying like squirrels in a
bid to be at his backs and
calls , every lady wanted to

have a bit of him , Just a
feel of his sturdy built will
do . His comrades wouldn't
trust him with their babes ,
even the married ones
amongst them couldn't
leave him alone with their
wives, it was that bad .

....
      ....
      ....

" O Michael honey , you are such a
handsome guy, I mean
every woman will kill to
have you "

Purred a young lady in her middle
thirties, her eyes harboured
a satisfied glint , the wide
grin wouldn't leave her well
sculptured face . She gave
Michael a wet kiss on his
lips and continued with her
talk .

" My husband never touches me
the way you do , gosh ! you
know every secret place of
a woman's body and you
are just nineteen , wow !
boy you are precocious in
every ramification , you are
a savvy"

Michael's only reply was a sweet
chuckle , he has become so
accustomed to the effusive
praises from the female

folks that he now either smile or chuckle his thank you.

"O ! my darling , my eyes have been on you ever since your first year in this university"

She mouthed salaciously and stroked his beards , her glance roaming the tendrils of hair on his chin.

" ha lydia lydia !

He arched his head and exclaimed in mock surprise .

"And you decided to make it known to me now that am in my final year "

" O ! Michael , what would you have me do , you were fresh into school , what would people say ?

"Ok lady lydia , guess i was still a fresher in my second and third year "

He replied sardonically.

"Not that Michael , everyone wil....."

"Does everyone have to know ? He bellowed in exasperation

"O Micheal , i am so so sorry , I just
felt I should give you some
time , so you won't freak
out when I approach you "

She explained with unalloyed calm

" O then that explains the unmerited
marks i get from you "

He said rather to himself

" Yes honey , I can't refuse you
nothing , you know I love
you so much , you are just
too beautiful and I hope am
not too old for you ?   She
quizzed

" What ! goodness gracious me !
Lydia you are just thirty
_five for Pete's sake , you
are just opportuned to be a
professor at a very young
age , a professor in
psychology and English for
that matter , shit ! baby you
are a Natural "

He said, with a tinge of sincerity .

" Wow Michael ! thanks "   Came
her elated reply , Her grin
was almost tearing her face
apart , She practically
thrusted her cute face into
his and at that moment ,
their mouth locked , the
kiss lingered for minutes

until She finally broke it and suddenly a frown plastered her face .

"What baby ?

He asked , obviously bewildered.

And She made a lame mistake by asking innocently .

" Michael darling , I have been wanting to ask you "

" Ask me What lydia?

" Michael isn't it strange ?

" What is strange baby ?

" That you never get to pull off your shirt in my presence , even during love making , you are always careful not to yank off your shirt, it's always plastered on your skin like a tattoo "

Michael stiffened and went rigid under her touch and for an awful moment the blissful atmosphere went sour with malevolence .Lydia noticed his awkward disposition and suddenly went frantic with worry .

" Errrmmm Michael did I say something wrong ?

His silence perturbed her and she was transported into a frenzy , her entire body started to twitch .

" Mich..ael are yo...u Alright ?

Came her confused stutter.

Michael suddenly jerked his head towards her , greeted her with a menacing glare and snarled .

" Woman ! you have flown too close to my Sun , you have spured my demons and now they have been stired awake "

Lydia shivered in panic , the dark look in his eyes bespoke pain and terror , it's something she has never seen before in their five months of sexual escapades, it was alien and perilous.

She immediately climbed out of the mattress and hurriedly put on her shoes and dress_ years of extensive study of psychology gave her the uncanny feeling that he must have gone nut and if she doesn't make dialogues with her legs , hail as heavy as rocks will pelt down on her savagely without remorse .

Lydia was about reaching for the door when Michael skillfully grabbed her by the arm and thundered at the zenith of his thick baritone with a glint of dark ire dancing in his eyes , it was as though a spirit possesed him at that moment .

" Hey you nosy woman ! the next time you pull a fast one on me again , I Will make sure I skin your hide, you bitch !

" Ye...sssss ye....sss"

She stuttered rather hurriedly , her eyes almost bulged out of their socket , her body was beaded with perspiration and her eyes already was blurred with mists of tears .

" Ca..n I g..o?

She stuttered again , looking at everywhere but his eyes.

" Yes yes bitch , you Can " Came his amused reply which was accompanied with a tinge of wicked chuckles

This startled the helpless woman and She jumped with a start
.

" O how I glory in the fear that comes running into their beautiful faces" He thought

" Now common baby , come give your baby boy a hug"

He said cheerfully asif what just transpired never happened .He spread out his sturdy arms hence awaited her lithe body to get submerged into his gallant bulk, She reluctantly went into his embrace , afraid that he might strangle her.

" Good woman, now you can go home and don't hesitate to drive home like the good girl that you are " He said with a smirk

"'Ok "

She said slowly and scurried out of the room like a squirrel. While walking through the dark passage of the big building , She hastened her footsteps and kept looking back, afraid that he might be following her .

On getting into her car She breath a deep sigh of relief and held the steering tightly so that her knuckles turned white .

" That guy is obviously a psychopath, gosh ! how can I be so oblivious of this fact all these months , O ! thank GOD am alive "

Again She let out a deep sigh and fired the car to life ....

EPISODE 7

A beautiful woman in her early 40s stood imperiously like a queen in front of her humongous mirror which over the years have become a close acquaintance and companion .

She smiled proudly at the reflection in the mirror , obviously happy with what She is seeing . Her expensive night gown was a sharp contrast to her fair skin color but a striking resemblance to her heart .

" Michael O Michael "   She purred softly

" Like your amorous father , you won't be able to resist me

tonight , you won't Michael
"

She muttered under her breath and walked slowly to her bed , She grabbed the big teddy bear which obviously Will clamour for freedom if it could talk , She began to talk to the immobile object as though it could hear her , her mouth pouted petulantly like that of a stubborn child .

" Michael sweetheart, am coming for you like I always do , but tonight we are gonna play our usual game , if you as much as try to resist , I Will inflict more pains on you with my whip and you are gonna get more ugly scars coupled with more terrible nightmares and mind you Michael , I have power over you , you can't fight back , you can't! hahahahahaha"

A wicked glint flashed in her eyes , she planted a kiss on the teddy bear's puffed cheeks and placed it gently on the bed .She slowly walked out of the room , the hem of her dress was reaching the ground like an over flowing wedding gown .

She gently opened the door of the room opposite hers and waltzed in , She stood arms akimbo , reveling at the sleeping handsome figure . Her hands suddenly flew to her mouth in shock and She continued to gawk at the sleeping figure asif she was expecting to see a boy instead of a man,   then suddenly she began to sob softly .

" O my ! that's my Eric, yes that's him ! he is back , he is back '"

'she muttered softly under her breath amidst sobs. She suddenly wiped her tears with the back of her right hand , she moved forward ,Sat down gently at the edge of the bed and reached out for the beautiful sleeping man who snored on in oblivion.

She slowly unbuttoned his shirt and began to caress his hairy chest , her dainty hands navigated the scars on his chest , her last gesture was accompanied   with   a mischievous wicked grin which danced a wierd move on her face .

" These scars are my work of art ,
you are my work of art ,
Michael baby "

She made to kiss his chest when the
handsome sleeping figure
suddenly jolted
awake , he stared at the crazy
wanton   woman   sitting
beside him and sighed with
a heavy pain in his heart
.He had dreaded coming
back home to his aunt.

" Aun...ty   it's   yo...u"   He
stuttered

"Fuck!   he muttered under his
breathe

" This bitch is here again , why do I
fear her so much , what
influence does she have
over me , why does she
have control over me , O !
even her presence weakens
me, shit! the bitch won't
even get old , why does she
always look so imperious
and beautiful like a queen ?
Thus came the tumult of
questions   that   played
games in his head .

" Hey ! mich , get a grip on yourself,
common   Michael,
remember you are the boss
now , stop panicking like a

twelve year old boy , you are even now stronger physically , just Chase the deranged bitch out of your room " His silent thoughts kept on rummaging his head

" Fuck ! this bitch lied to me, but she seemed so contrite on the phone the day she called , the wanton told me she just had a surgery and is recuperating at home , then how come a sick bitch still wants sex. Definitely she must be a dark witch for having a strong grip on me , why did I ever come back home to this bitch? for Pete's sake am now an adult , O how I wish she really had that surgery and just die " His crazy thoughts lingered

" Ah! this gutsy bitch used jazz on me, I just hate her guts, this feeling of paranoia and weakness I get whenever I see her must leave me today , I must show this black witch that am not a kid anymore and can no more be enslaved in her madness " He concluded within himself

" O LORD pls save me from her evil claws " He quickly added to his thoughts.

" Haaaaaaaa haaaaaaa"

The crazy lady chuckled in wicked delight , obviously amused at his discomfiture. Asif reading his thoughts, she said .

" The same grip I had on your father, I also have it on you honey , can't you see ? you both belong to me , you both are drawn to me like a moth to a flame , you arc caught up in my web honey and honey I just missed my sexual escapades with you , I didn't go through any surgery ok , that was only a facade to draw you home to me and you came running home like a cheetah because you love your aunt , just like your father .Can't you see honey , you belong to me "

" No aunty, i don't belong to you , am not a twelve_ year old boy anymore , am now a full fledged man . You told me you are dying , I don't care if it's a pseudo surgery but it Will give me profound joy to see you die though and rot in hell you crazy bitch!

He bellowed rather hurriedly in a feisty manner but averted her gaze as though he was scared of her , his voice was raw with emotions and tinged with fear .

" O ! my !

Priscilla gasped , Obviously feigning surprise at his sharp retort , deep down she could see through him , she knew it took him every modicum of courage to retort .

'"Hmmm our little teeny weeny Michael now talks back at his aunt, it's intriguing though "

She said with mock admiration hence teasing him

" But baby Mich.........

Michael fumed with rage , his teeth was seething with anger , he became pepper red at being called a baby .She ignored his angry gestures and continued with her tirades .

" Do you know that you are such an A1 bastard! hahaha, you think I don't know about your sexual escapades with older rich women and how you man handle women , hahaha, you see honey , you are a pervert and psychopath , we are one , we are both monsters hahaha "

Michael glowered at her in indignation , films of perspiration clinged obdurately to his scarred skin.

" Aunty please get out of my room before I Do somethingdrastic to you !

" Haaaaaaaa haaaaaaaaaaaaaa " She let out a mocking and annoying laughter and almost fell to the floor in a fever of excitement .

" Am the only family you have got honey in the whole world , you are addicted to me baby just as your father was , you can't hurt me baby "

Tides of anger welled up within Michael , he gave her that menacing glare of his , if only looks could kill .

Emboldened   by
malevolence and ire , he
shouted .

" You shameless bitch !

"'yea of course , I know that all right
, I was your father's bitch
baby "   She   spewed,
obviously unnerved by his
angry retorts .

" You think I would fall at your feet
like a penitent lover , just
like when I was a kid , you
queen of bitches! You
made me do unimaginable
things at a very tender age,
I would so much love You
to run to hell where You
rightfully belong , like right
now in a hurry , You witch
! You messed up my entire
life !

He climbed out of the bed and
waltzed out of the room
rather hurriedly .. Priscilla
stared wide eyed at the
door   and   grinned
sheepishly .

" Hmmmm he now walks out on me
"

She placed her right hand on her jaw
and looked heaven word ,
asif trying to decipher the

strength behind his new found courage .

....
....
....
....

Priscilla Stumped out of the room after her angry nephew and found him seething in anger in the couch , she slowly walked towards him and Sat beside him but he shifted slightly , she ignored him and started to carress his beards, this made him to wince, obviously irritated by her touch .

She got irked by his angry gestures and did as though she wanted to remove a spec from his eyes but instead blest him with a piping hot slap . Michael jumped with a start and held his face firmly ,he didn't showcase any sign of pain, he was already used to his aunt's uncanny gestures towards him .

"And how dare you walk out on me , you little brat ! I can see you have grown wings you Stupid boy,! i gave you everything, I gave you a standard education and a good life , you bastard! you practically lived in affluence under my roof , you are an ungrateful bra...."

" You lie ! you black witch ! besides I know you killed my parent , it's something only you can do , bitch !   Thus came his sharp interruption .

His whole body started to twitch vigorously for fear gnawed at him , fear for the cryptic crazy woman who is always on black . He suddenly regretted ever spitting out those last words of his .

" What if she kills me too with her voodoo?   He thought frantically.

Priscilla gasped in shock , his last words really hit her hard this time like the report of a gun , like a flash she ran towards the door upstairs , bolted it and dashed into her
room, it was as though those her crazy demons have all woken with vigour.

Michael knew what was coming but surprisingly stood rooted

on a spot as though he was
been controlled by a remote
. Priscilla came out shortly
, clutching a whip. When
she got to where he stood ,
she stopped on her track
and gave the whip an
impressive stare as she
always do before using it
on him When he was little
and defenseless .

" Hey honey , you know what this
does to you right , this will
forever be the death of you
"

She started to stroke the whip with
the tip of her finger and for
an awful moment she was
lost to the world around
her, it was as though the
whip was communicating
with her in a cryptic
language .

" This whip is a totem" She purred

The   very sight of the dreadful
object made Michael to
reminisce on his terrible
childhood and for the
fleetest moment he looked
once again like a twelve _
year old boy , he took a
retreating step whilst
shaking like a perturbed
leaf . He remembered the
dreadful object like it was

yesterday , he remembered how She used it on him every single night , how She ravenously lick his blood after registering myriad of hits on his body with the wicked looking " koboko" (whip) which makes him dread the holidays during his versity days. For a nano second , he seemed like the teeny weeny boy of yesterday .

Priscilla's attention was suddenly diverted from the whip , She jerked her head and looked towards him , She caught a trace of fear in his eyes and smiled knowingly with a wicked glint , obviously amused .

She decided to utilize this opportunity and imperiously tilted her head upward so that She meets his fearful gaze for he was provocatively tall . Confident that he would surely cave in this time , She yanked off her customary black nightie which rendered her provocatively naked and bare .

"'Now Michael darling , you Will do to me what your father did to my body , you Will touch me this moment and unravel the mysteries of my body "

Michael shifted slightly from one foot to the other and continuously shook his head , he was obviously in a frenzy .

" 'No aunty ! I won't do this anymore , am now a man ! a man !

He interjected

Knowing him too well , Priscilla still discerned fear and uncertainty in his eyes, emboldened by his disposition , she moved towards him and made to touch his groin but he quickly yanked off her hand asif it scalded him.

" You demon possessed woman ! why don't you leave me be ! if you don't leave me be I Will expose you to the world and ruin your political career !

He shouted in exasperation and he seemed like he meant it . His masculinity was worn around him like pride which fascinated the baffled woman , for the very first time she felt his threat like a sword drawn to her heart , her heart suddenly became a bloated dessolute wreck and at that moment , she lost the ability to speak and silence ensued in the room .

Her disposition bolstered his wavering confidence and like a silver blade , he cut through the silence that was threatening to eat up the house .

" And aunty "

He moved slightly towards her , ganer courage and yanked the whip "koboko" off her twitching grip , he threw it on the couch and just like a flash , that alien dark look suddenly made way into his eyes, they were artic like snow. He grabbed her hands violently and said rather too harshly .

" You have flown too close to my Sun , you spured the demons in me and now they have been stired awake "

Priscilla froze and stared at him , her mouth agape with shock .

She obviously have not seen that dark look before , she blinked for the umpteenth time and managed to find her bearing .

" O jeez ! Mich..ael you have rea...lly go...ne out of char...acter , i trai..ned you to be cultur...ed"

She stuttered in panic , shifted slightly and avoided his glare .

" Look at kettle calling pot black " He snorted

On realizing that his resolve have hardened and he now seemed in control of himself , She decided to utilize an all too cheap tactic just to elicit compassion from him .,she eyed him again to see his reaction . Amidst her pretense sobs , She started to speak seductively .

" O baby , you have really changed towards your aunt, you know am going through difficulties in my upcoming campaign , you never came back home since your third year in school , I miss you so much honey , just hold me tight and touch me in every contours of my being, come touch my breast and feel its soothing softness "

" You wanton ! I am not moved by your charades you disgustful bitch , you disgust me , gosh ! He spat

"'why can't I just hurt you ! I really can't stifle the urge to twist your neck so you would have easy passage to hell where you rightfully belong ! He snarled

"'why is it a herculean task for me to just kill this bitch like I have always done to bitches like her, what's really holding me back ? He quizzed himself through his thought .

Emboldened by anger at not being able to prefer answers to the tumult of questions running through his head , he snarled at her again .

" Trust me to expose you , you shrew !

Still naked, Priscilla suddenly realized his resolve has hardened and she can't win him over anymore, she went wild with rage and gave him a piping hot slap across the face and was about to administer another one when he suddenly grabbed her by the arm and violently pushed her, she fell with a thud on the floor and let out a high pitched cry.

" I dont want to kill you , don't push me you dark witch !   He thundered

" You ungrateful brat !   She screamed

Michael suddenly became charged , he yanked the whip off the couch ,savagely dragged her by the hair and pulled her violently to the door . Her deafening scream gingered him to violence , he pushed her out of the house like a rag , threw the whip after her and violently closed the door hence she was susceptible to cold for she was provocatively naked save for the shawl which she quickly grabbed from the couch before he threw her out .

" You A1 bastard !

Came her deafening scream which was akin to that of a pole cat. She banged the door with every strength and will power and wouldn't quit cussing at him.

" A1 bitch

He responded and spat

EPISODE 8

"JESUS !

Thus Came the raucous exclamation of the shocked beautiful lady .Her legs were transfixed to a spot and her eyes were almost bulging out of their socket , her hands spontaneously flew to her mouth and tears filled her eyes. She suddenly recovered her bearing and muttered under her breathe.

" This is unbelievable, preposterous , nasty and disgusting , no child should go through all you went through , baby your story is really touching "

Michael was brought back to reality from his sad reverie by her

words, he jerked slightly
and blinked for the
umpteenth time, his red
eyes met her shocked ones
and he muttered inadibly ,
making Natasha to strain
her neck towards his mouth
.

"Tasha, that's all there is to tell ,
that's my true life story "

He bent his head slightly , a gesture
that showed that he was
contrite , then he
remarked , obviously shamefaced .

"Believe me Tasha, I regretted every
nasty things I did to those
women , I am a husk of a
man , I did terrible things
Tasha, Will you leave me
after all you've heard today
?

" O no sweetheart i am going
nowhere honey "   Came
her teary reply

She glanced at him and felt his
scrutiny of her heart ,
suddenly she became
inflamed ,not at him but at
the world and aunty
Priscilla . She touched him
slightly on the shoulder, a
gesture which She felt Will
assure him of her presence ,
then She said with a trace

of malevolence in her voice
.

" I never knew Honourable Priscilla Drake Ejiofor is a beast . She frequents my neighbourhood and doesn't hesitate to decorate my community with wads of Naira notes, She provided a youth scholarship scheme for my community and sponsored some of us through the university"

She suddenly stopped talking and sighed heavily , She took Michael's right hand into hers and gave it an affectionate squeeze . She further gave him a look that said " Should I continue ? Michael read meaning to her look and nodded in the affirmative . Natasha continued talking in regret and appeared crestfallen .

" She created business opportunitdoes for others , I benefited from all her benevolence and immediately took a liking to her and made her my number one role model, I was also so stupid to have allotted prominence and confer status to her via my media prowess"

She paused again but Michael nodded in a bid to permit her to continue her story .

" O my GOD ! I just realized how stupid I was to envisage her as a mother figure "

Michael's head jerked towards hers, he let out a surprised whistle , his mouth a grim line , he remarked .

" Tasha honey , next time be careful of what you wish for , that bitch is a very crazy and ambitious woman , she did all that because she is a politician and is in desperate need of your votes , it's politics darling , pure politics "

He enveloped her delicate fingers into his and continued with a voice that was tainted with sorrow , not sparing Natasha a minute to talk , it was as though he needed to pour out all the ire that was locked in his heart .

" Anytime she lost an election to a more certified candidate she goes pepper red with rage and inflicts malevolent pain on me with the wipe then Will go ahead to have sex with me right until she satisfies her crazy urge. Tasha she is a very insane woman , very sick in the head "

He thrusted his face into hers and touched her soft cheeks , he kissed her lightly in the lips ,removed his hands from her face and continued .

"Every night , she beats me with the whip , feed on my blood like a vampire then have sex with me whenever am unconscious"

He nodded his head as though he pitied himself and continued .

" Tasha, I grew up seeing women as pieces of trash , I hated them and treated them very badly , all thanks to that whore"

"O baby ! She is indeed crazy , I mean what woman Will have sex with an underaged boy"

She uttered in bewilderment.

Michael ignored her question and continued.

"I gained admission into a private university at my very first try , at first She was reluctant to sponsor me but miraculously changed her mind and made me promise to always come back home during the holidays"

He stopped midways, gave Natasha his best smile as though to tell her not to pity him .

" She is very good at predicting my next moves, She knew I would feel reluctant to return to her so She did the silliest thing and sent her chauffeur to always pick me up after every semester"

He paused and sighed heavily

" In my third year , I stopped following the chauffeur home , She became infuriated and stopped sponsoring me in school but before then I had been dating rich female lecturers who showered me with money even without billing them "

He suddenly paused again but this time around clasped her hands into his as an affectionate gesture .

"'I knew I was on my own so I did the most sensible thing and started a cyber cafe business in school and Mich enterprise was born " He said rather proudly with his chest almost puffing out

.

" Before graduation , I had become so rich and never really bothered about her until one faithful day ,she beeped me and congratulated me on my success , she lied to me that she had a surgery and was recuperating at home and goodness gracious me ! Tasha she sounded so contrite and reassured me that she have turned a New leaf "

Michael suddenly stopped talking , He placed his hand in her hair and removed a thin blue thread , an after effect of the struggle she had while trying to put on her cloth . He let out a smile as though he just did something great and continued talking .

"' One part of me just wanted her to die, the other part of me wanted to affirm her claims of turning a New leaf , so I decided to go see her and reassured myself that am no longer the scared little boy . When I got home , I was willing to forgive her but to my chagrin the incorrigible bitch haven't changed a tiny bit , she tried her usual tricks on me that fateful night , I stifled the urge to beat her to death , I just did the sanest thing and threw her out of the house "

"O Michael, you have really suffered a lot , I was so stupid to think that she attributed to your success today " She remarked , silent play of emotions found the elegant lines of her beautifull face , he planted a soft kiss on her lips to tell her it wasn't her fault .

" I was never lucky with serious relationships and I always went for older and rich ladies, I changed women like cloth , it's either i scare them away with my awkward mannerisms when they start becoming too curious about me or I beat them up "

He thrusted his face again into hers and gave her a soft long look , his heart was singing a rhythmic melodious tune and they beat so earnestly for her .

" But you are one different woman Tasha, like my aunt your presence weakens me but in an all too different way that flutters my heart , the very first day I set my eyes on you at my company's press conference was the very first day I felt love . I immediately knew that I must keep you , I never wanted to scare you away with my strange mannerisms so after we got introduced I started seeing a shrink "

"O baby , all for me ?

She asked softly , her eyes dancing with love for him .

" yes honey , you are one special woman , if you had noticed, anytime you get me angry I tend to walk out on you to prevent myself from hurting you baby but today I didn't know what came over me , honey am so sorry for being unreasonably harsh on you

, please sweetheart don't leave me '"

He said shamefaced, obviously for previously hitting her . Natasha suddenly began to sob and uttered no word of reproach , her voice threatening to rise again into a despairing wail. Scarcely able to stop sobbing , she planted her misty face into his already opened sturdy embrace .

Her inability to stop sobbing transported Michael into a frenzy , he quickly freed her from his embrace and knelt down before her like a penitent lover , he rested his head on her laps and joined in the cue of sobs , he lifted his head and made to kiss her feet when she quickly held him back .

" No Mich , don't do that ! She bellowed in panick .

" No Tasha, just let me kiss your feet, you are my queen for life , please don't leave me "

" O no ! Michael I know you are a good man , I won't go anywhere without you , GOD has really been your helper all these years , he will never forsake you "

"AMEN "   Came his soft reply

Natasha suddenly jerked her head towards his his and asked with a glint of curiosity .

" So Michael , how about the craze woman , she no longer trends on social media for the past two years being who she is , so Mich where is she?

Michael stiffened and she discerned fear .

" O Michael not again , we do need to find her so she Will be exposed to the world and Will explain herself , she need not bother you again in every ramification, Mich let's just end this fear and shame " Natasha pondered

"ok Tasha , she has finally gone crazy " He surrendered

" What do you mean ? Quizzed the puzzled lady .

Michael gave her a long look and for an awful moment , Natasha thought he won't talk .

" Apparently she is raving in madness in a psychiatric home "

" O my !

Natasha exclaimed ......

EPISODE 9

An awkward looking entity stood arms akimbo and immobile like a statue , her eyes always bulging out now and then was fixed so intently on the rather large mahogany door that separated her from the outside world .

Her once smooth long black hair now a striking semblance to dreadlocks carried a Dusty film that adorned her cheeks like talcum powder and it hung down in unwashed unruly black strands .

Her eyes cryptic like password was bereft of life and everything good , they stayed transfixed to the rather huge mahogany door , never blinking , never flinching . She suddenly smiled slightly which transported a dark twist to her mouth , it made her suddenly look old and mangy . She heard a door click open from afar and her once beautiful face suddenly lit up with a enigmatic grin , sounds of hurried footsteps followed which made her to shift uncomfortably on her heels .

She suddenly started to mouth unintelligible words that only mad persons would understand . like a flash , the door to her new world suddenly flew open and her eyes became alert like a cat's. She gawked at the three intruders who all stood at a vantage point in a bid to evade any of her funny moves .

" Mr Michael, we are in what we would call a precarious situation,   right now She would be needing your fervent supports and prayers since you are the only family she's got "

Remarked Dr Ibe, obviously breaking the silence that

was threatening to eat up the room .

Michael only half heard what the doctor said , he stood transfixed on a spot and stared in horror and unbelievably at the deranged lady , her disoriented body and disheveled hair made a different pang to hit him .

"Errmmmm Doctor I hope she isn't completely mad?   He nervously replied

The crazy lady caught wind of his last words and suddenly jerked her head towards him. Her face twisted into a sneer , she arched her head and shouted whilst pointing her haggard fingers at Michael's direction . " You ! Eric , you are the mad one here , you Eric , you ! you ! you , Eric youuuuuuuuu!!

Her breathes caught jaggedly , they were as sharp as the report of a gun , the blaze in her eyes was a discernable glow . She suddenly looked at the direction of the lady standing beside Michael and jumped in surprise as though she was oblivious of her presence since they barged into her territory .

" Hey! you ! you little girl standing beside my Eric , go get me chilled water now !

She bellowed her command which was almost a semblance to her old imperious self .

Natasha Jumped in fear , a flicker of uncertainty crossed her face , She looked at the doctor and he nodded and wanted to say " If you love yourself ma'am just get her the water so we will all leave this room in one piece as we all came in " instead he pleaded .

" Please ma'am , the water Is in the other room , get it for her specifically in a glass cup"

He emphasized the word " GLASS" for yes sir trouble will ensue If She doesn't bring the water in s glass cup .

Natasha quickly nodded and scurried put of the room , She came back gingerly with a cup full of water , emboldened by the doctor's nod She walked toward the crazy lady in palpable fear and handed over the

cup full of water to her .
The crazy lady grabbed the
water from Natasha's
twitching hands so that a
little quantity of water
splattered on the floor .

" Clumsy little girl !   Careless
Nanita !   The crazy lady
snarled

This made Natasha to retreat with a
jump and found herself in
Michael's sturdy arms,She
melted like wax in his
strong eembrace and sighed
deeply in unalloyed relief
.The crazy lady glared at
them for a while and
looked at the cup as though
the content contains poison
, she shrugged and
surprisingly slurped down
the water hungrily , it
coursed down her throat ,
not a single meagre
swallow but a flow of gulp
after gulp of paradise . She
let out a sheepish
contented smile and gave
Natasha an all too brief
smiles asif to say " Thank
you "

Natasha smiled back in cue , in a bid
to tell the crazy lady that
She understood her gesture
. Natasha made to collect
the cup when the crazy

lady gave out an unlady like snort, She smiled slightly with a conspiratory twist to her mouth and pretended to give the cup to Natasha but suddenly smashed the glass cup and let out a strange giggle . Natasha screamed and again found herself in Michael's strong arms, this time around ,She was panting in his strong embrace .

"This was how I smashed Eric and my little bitchy baby sister Nanita, I have been raving with madness right from my mother's womb , hahahaha,it I who orchestrated the car accident that took their lives after I arrived home from the state . I did something tricky to their tyre just before they embarked on a journey , so now you see Michael my handsome little nephew , it was I who killed your parent so am raving mad !hahahahah"

"What !

Natasha shouted in terror ..

Michael's hands clenched into a tight angry fist , his whole being was seething wiith ire, her words penetrated his befuddled state and drove home , his eyes shone like thunder and suddenly metamorphosed into an angry glow , there was murder in those eyes . He made to lurch forward towards his derangedy aunt , probably to register an angry slap across her face when he suddenly felt the cool hands of the doctor on his left shoulder .

He stoped on his track , heaved angry sighs and roared like an anger lion amidst tears , his voice was crowded with emotions he couldn'tcontrol .

"Aunty why ! What have my parent ever done to you ? What have I ever done to you ? Why did you destroy us ?Aunty why !

The crazy lady ignored his outburst , she licked her parched lips and said coyly , oblivious of the emotional effect her words have on her poor nephew .

" And I would so much love to kill you both , just watch and see how I do it "

"GOD forbid , you would do no such thing ma'am" Natasha remarked in a feisty manner, her arms akimbo and her eyes afire with determination but deep down fear gnawed at her , her heart pounded so hard she could scarcely breath.

"hahahaha , you little brats , just watch and see me do wonders "

This infuriated Michael , he stifled the urge to charge towards her and punch her on the face but instead he remarked angrily "You mad woman ! right now you reek of madness, you should be reeling in shame, not figuring how to shed more blood "

He removed his handkerchief from his back pocket and cleaned the beads of sweart that's threatening to blur his vision and scowled at the crazy lady , crowned with anger he continued .

" You are obviously paying for all the ruthless things you have done in the past , you have finally met your Waterloo , every evil you committed has boomeranged on you "

Natasha held his arm and made to lead him out of the room when he suddenly jerked her hand out of his impulsively , tear tricked done his eyes for nothing could hurt more than the agony that lodged somewhere near his solar plexus every time he remembered the disgusting activities she made him carry out at a tender age . Unnerved by Natasha's Silent plea to eave the room , he continued .

"Karma had finally caugh......"

" O !just shut it Eric !

The crazy lady rudely interrupted Michael and to the shock surprise of everyone she immediately fished out a small sized pistol from the pocket of her hospital garment .Every in the room went into a frenzy , Natasha knew Michael would be her first target , she became powerfully uncomfortable and staggered in shock , her hands flew to her mouth in Shock.

The crazy lady fired the gun at Michael's direction , fortunately fior Michael , Natasha had already calculated her move , she quickly grabbed Michael's arms and pushed him out of harm's way and he fell on the floor with a loud thud , this made the crazy lady to miss her first shot .

The crazy lady screamed in defeat like a wounded pole cat, a look of something savage shone in her eyes , they were as dark as the night , the frown she wore on her face was the size of Lagos . Before everyone could even get their bearing ,the crazy lady angrily lurched towards Natasha's direction and like a flash she hit Natasha on the head with the edge of the gun , Natasha screamed , fell on the floor with a loud thud and became unconscious.

Overwhelmed with alarm , Dr ibe ran out in desperate need for help .

Her face set and herd ,the deranged lady gave Michael a look that struck terror In his soul .The confused Michael quickly stood up from the floor and ran towards the almost lifeless body of the love if his life , he went frantic with worry and made to lift Natasha up when the crazy lady pounced on him .She had pounced on him myriad of times so she gloried in this one .

Her gesture made Michael to lose balance , he fell back on the floor and like a dark entitity she was all over him .

"Where In tarnation am I going to get help from ? surely this crazy lady Is really abetted by some strong forces O! LORD please spare my life , help me LORD, I don't want to die young " Indeed those were Michael's desperate prayers ..

Oblivious of what was running through Michael's head , the deranged woman kept up with her madness , she scratched his face violently and rented his shirt into shreds whilst ranting .

"Hahahaha , my little Eric , do you remember this game , now you are powerless , I have power over you and your father , and if I don't have you , no one can , I decide who lives "

She suddenly became calm and stopped talking, she began to lick the wounds on Michael's scratched face and was lost to the whole surrounding around her .Michael smartly took advantage of her sudden calmness , he skillfully and quietly grabbed the gun which was lying in wait beside her , he made to fling it away when she suddenly became alert and dragged it from his unstable grip .

She was about to place her hand on the trigger when Michael angrily made a mistake of registering a thunderous slap across her face . Her screams rented the air and it was as though Michael's sudden slap empowered her for she suddenly became more powerful and started to scratch his face again with her rather long fingers but this time around , she was more intent .

Angry red blood spilled out of Michael's face into different directions, she was bent on sucking the life out of him like a typical vampire and for a nano second Michael thought sincerely for the first time they she really is a vampire for she have sucked his blood all his life .

Michael' stoically received the extricating pain and the scratches though now weak from losing too many blood , long years of receiving scratches from her rather too long finger nails has made him mmune to pains .

Michael wouldn't give up though slightly weak , so fight ensued and they started to roll over each other whilst both dragging the dangerous object (gun) , it was quite a
scenario. Finally and Miraculously, Michael rolled over her and made hard effort to relief the gun off her tight grip , careful not to perturb the trigger .

The struggle to collect the gun from her hands made the crazy lady to spontaneously rest her armed hands on her tummy so that the mouth of the gun is dangerously facing her stomach whilst he struggled to rid her hands off the trigger of the gun which she stubbornly held tightly with all seriousness and with a strength that perplexed Micheal.

"Gosh !I i what to save the crazy bitch ! if only she would just allow me have this fucking gun so I would discard it , holy moses! the mouth of the fucking thing is facing her tummy ! stubborn mad bitch!

He muttered under his breath in exasperation and confusion.

The crazy lady was becoming impatient and agitated , she suddenly went went with rage and screamed , Michael got distracted and slightly loosened the grip he had on her, oblivious of this fact , the stubborn deranged woman mistakenly pulled the trigger which Michael have been desperately preventing from being pulled by her crazy hands .

Silence engulfed the rather too strange room, Michael stiffened at the shot of the pistol, he immediately knew the report of the gun didn't go well .The nurses ,patients, doctors and even police officers who all cowardly stood in vantage point watching the crazy scenario in horror all trouped in when they realized that the orchestrator of danger has mistakenly taken her own life .

Michael couldn't register what just happened, he made to say something when he suddenly felt air swiftly rush into his mouth , he gasped and swallowed his saliva which thawed obdurately at his innards . He stifled a groan and couldn't think properly for his body felt like tar , thick and heavy with injury and pain.

The once lit room now bathed with Michael's angry red blood tainted the atmosphere , it was akin to the devil's sanctuary . Michaels vision went blurry with thick blood , he closed his eyes and suddenly became oblivious of the happenings around him .

"He isn't dead , he is still breathing "

A voice shoted

" Holy Christ ! He lookes beat "

Another voice exclaimed ....

EPOSODE 10

"Dr jude, this is the Angel I want to get married to , please meet Natasha Chimamanda Nwadi , She is a journalist "

Michael Remarked with pride and a wide grin that almost almost split his face into two , he wouldn't even look at the doctor's smilling face and wouldn't stop staring at Natasha .His face lit up like Christmass and he added rather too shyly like a secondary school boy but still not giving the shrink as a much as a glance

"She completes my world "

He suddenly became oblivious of the shrink presences and made to Kiss the puzzled and embarrassed Natasha when the doctor suddenly interrupted his romantic gestures when he noticed Natasha helpless state .

"Hmmmmmm ehnnnn hmmmmmm"

Dr jude mockingly cleared his throat

The unabashed Michael nodded his head apologetically and remarked .

"So sorry about that doctor , Natasha please meet my Shrink Dr Jude Okoro"

Natasha met the doctor's eyes shyly and exposed her best polite smile , She held out her hands and shook his outstretched hands .

"it's a pleasure meeting you sir and thank you sir for shaping my man into a better version of himself "

"No mention ma'am, it's definitely GOD'S doing not mine " He replied

" And don't forget ma'am, you equally contributed to his well being "

He chirped in as an afterthought and winked , Michael's and the shrink's eyes locked and they smiled knowingly at each other .Then He said to Michael .

" And you gentleman , i hope you still forgive your aunt even in death"

Michael suddenly stiffened and his countenance changed , the shrink decided to ignore him and continued .

" Mrs Priscilla Drake Ejofor had a brain tumour when she was twelve and had an operation, the operation went well but years later , your grandparent discovered that her brain got affected again and it resulted to a psychological issue "

He searched Michael's eyes for any trace of curiousity and smiled when he discovered one amidst Michael's disapproving frown

"My father happened to be the surgeon that operated on

her alongside his colleagues and thorough investigations showed that though the operation was successful , but your aunt went ahead to hit her head on a block a week after she was discharged from the hospital whilst playing with her friends , this led to more issues "

The curious duo both looked puzzled and inclined their ears to the doctor's story . The doctor realized he had got their rapt attention and continued .

"Base on my findings some years back , I discovered that she stabbed her twin sister to death at the age of 18 whom she accused her of snatching her boyfriend . your grandparent tried as much as possible to conceal the incident and termed it as being suicidal so as to protect their political interest .

"IO boy !

Natasha whistled I'm shock

"So that bitch had a twin "

Michael muttered under his breathe , he blanched at the shrink's short story and the coffee he was drinking thawed at his innards ,he stifled a grown and his head felt like it was being hit wit a heavy rod , a chill ran through his spine like So many spider's icy feet .

"How can I forgive a woman that led trouble to me line Judas to the LORD, a woman who made me a psychopath and a monster , she made me do terrible things   she made me live a lovelorn life "   Michael thought aloud

"You just have to Michael , you have to , I mean she is dead and gone , what difference does it Make ?   Natasha remarked . Her eyes was soft with love for him , her voice was wholesome and warm like new milk .

"You really have to son "   The doctor chirped in

Michael looked at their pleading eyes and looked heaven ward asif prayer for divine intervention , he started d to pray in his heart , his stoic scarred face was painted with past pains .

"In am nothing but a shell , oh GOD put whatever you want inside of me , Give me the strength to love on without these pains , forgive me LORD and give me the heart to forgive "

Natasha and the shrink both gawked at him in bewilderment.

"Errrrm my love are u ok ?   The puzzled Natasha asked

Michael slowly came out of his reverie , he looked at her for a minute and didn't say a word , she stared back , wide eyes in anticipation . He finally spoke

" Tasha I have made up my mind "

"What !

She exclaimed

"No I mean I have made up my Mind to forgive my dead aunt after all the crazy things she did to me "

"Phew ! isn't GOD awesome ?

Natasha whistled in relief , her face was afire with happiness

and she was able to breath
at though something hard
around her heart had been
cracked open .

"very good my boy , I am very
proud of you ," Remarked
the elated shrink who was
obviously beaming like
someone who just won a
Jack pot..

A trace of a shy smile traveled
across Michael's handsome
face

"Now baby , will you marry me ?
Michael asked

He Knelt down and fished out a ring
from his rather too
expensive tailored suit
pocket with hands that
knew what they were doing
and held out a ring towards
her

"Good gracious me ! Exclaimed the
elated Natasha , a fever of
excitement rushed through
her veins . Michael still on
his knees , ring in hand
dreaded her response and
for a fleetest moment he
thought she was going to
refuse him and caught his
breath. But she giggled her
response deliciously like a
young bride

"I yes , yes honey , I Will marry you Mr Michael Eric Okafor"

"Oh THANK GOD"

Dr Jude muttered under his breast in sweet relief .
"

"THANK GOD

Michael repeated as though he was on cue with his shrink, he heaved a deep sigh of relief and beamed , his heart was summersaulting with love for the lady he just proposed to .He went ahead to place the expensive ring in her dainty finger and further enveloped her possesively into a tight hug like a child would do to its mother .

He freed her from his embrace , held her lovely sculptured face and stared lovingly at them , he released his killer smile and hugged her again , all his rough edges forgotten .

" Perfect " The elated shrink shouted in a fever of excitement , the grin on his face almost demarcation his face .

" Merci Doctor "   Natasha gracefully replied in her fiancees sturdy embrace .

"It's GOD',s doing my dear , It's GOD's doing "

Dr Jude replied heartily , the grin never leaving his face , He winked at Michael and Michael reciprocated with a huge smile that he reckoned Will never depart from face for life.............